Tarriance

An Anthology of

Stories, Poems and Memoirs

Published 2017 by Stratford Scribes

www.stratfordscribes.btck.co.uk

Copyright © 2017 Stratford Scribes

Taxi Rides with Daniel and Farm Elegy first published in 'Quintet and other Poets,' October 2015 by Cinnamon Press.

Chain Link first published in The Cannon's Mouth, Cannon Poets Quarterly, Issue 50, December 2013 by Cannon Poets.

ISBN: 978-1546640974

Introduction

Now entering its twelfth year, Stratford Scribes is an informal and supportive writing group. Based in South Warwickshire and meeting weekly, it caters for a range of writers from beginners to published authors. It is facilitated by Cathy Whittaker, who has been tutoring in Creative Writing for a number of years.

Tarriance is an anthology of stories, poems and memoirs written by the current members of the group.

We hope you will enjoy tarrying a while in our company.

Index   **Page**

Author Biographies

Life's Pages

I see the shelves of books so brightly bound,
whose stories have enraptured me for years,
a wall of pages hedging me around
making me laugh or moving me to tears.
Always at hand, comforting me without sound,
drowning my sorrows, calming all my fears.

When as a child the darkness held such fears
and feet caught in sheets made me suppose them bound,
my first books, fitting for my tender years,
dispelled the ogres I believed around.
The stuff of nightmares, terrifying me to tears,
crept round my bed, stopping my every sound.

In teenage days, with bedroom filled with sound,
when spots or puppyfat formed my major fears,
when dreams were University or even commune bound,
when the future stretched ahead in endless years,
fresh favourite books began to pile around
and new great heroes brought my ready tears.

At University frustration brought my tears,
hand thumping desk became the only sound.
Examination results were ever-present fears –
would I in disgrace be homeward bound?
But my textbooks proved my friends in all those years
and my 2:2 degree is good to see around.

When married my books were too many to have around
but pruning them brought forth fresh burst of tears.
I fetched them back from shops without a sound
and hid them away, amid discovery fears.
How could they be for charity disposal bound
when they had bolstered my spirits through my formative years?

Now all alone and stricken in my years
my books are a comfort, good to have around.
Once more with remembered pleasure and soft tears
they bring me joy, with laughter the only sound.
In long sleepless nights they once more calm my fears,
these old familiar tales in board or leather bound.

My bound companions, solace of the years,
ever around me through life's joys and fears.
We're all no longer sound, yet why waste tears?

Gwen Zanzottera

Lost Summer

September sun beats down on my head. The marrow weighs heavy in my hands. I tuck it under my arm and wipe away the trickle of sweat that runs across my face. I love the harvest.

This year we have been blessed with an Indian Summer. I watch as Jessie leans forward to cut another sun-kissed squash from its mother plant. Her deft movements have a rhythm and grace all their own. It must be six or seven weeks since she arrived, looking for work to tide her over the summer months.

'My Grandad used to have an allotment. I know all about growing veg.'

Tall, slim and confident, I take her on there and then. She hasn't failed me. This year promises to be the most fruitful yet.

I stand and gaze at the golden orbs covering the fields, at the feathered corn reaching skywards. Jessie places her squash in the work-worn wheelbarrow. She sees me watching her.

'Taking a break?' Her face splits into a wide grin. I take my marrow and lie it next to the squash.

'We're nearly done here. Would you like a cool beer?'

She shakes her head, corkscrew ginger curls bouncing over her shoulders.

'You have one. I left them in the box in the shade.'

She points to the trees that border our field.

'I'll cut the rest of the squash.'

I know she's telling me I need to rest. That, at my age, I shouldn't do too much. I want to shout that I'm not old. I can remember my summer.

I wander to the trees, open a bottle and take a mouthful. She works fast and soon the barrow threatens to tip, the pile of squash and marrows is so high. The rewards of autumn. She comes to me.

'All done.' She smiles. 'I suppose that's my work finished. The fields are empty. You must be pleased to have the food ready to sell so early.'

I wonder if I am. I say nothing.

'If you could pay me today, I'll be off in the morning. I might have enough to get to Africa now.'

She picks up her cardigan, slings it over her shoulders and heads for the gate. Away from me, away from the harvest, back to her summer.

I return to the wheelbarrow and lift the largest marrow from the top of the pile. September sun beats down on my head. The marrow weighs heavy in my hands.

Julie Fulton

Which Way the Land Lies

There is still a cattle shed, a farm gate and a rutted lane. Along the track, some distance from the road, there is a new house where the old farmhouse used to be. It is on the outskirts of the village, a short distance from where Nannie Brooks once lived, in a red corrugated tin bungalow with Uncle Walt. His hands and face black from the sacks of coal he carried and delivered on his bent back.

Often, on fine afternoons, my mother would put us in the big pram, my brother sitting one end and me the other and, with my oldest brother at her side, she would take us for a walk. We would go past the Manor House and along the turnpike where the chestnut trees grew. At the Church, we would cross the road to Little London Green. Occasionally, a car would pass, but more often we would meet a herd of cows on their way to the milking sheds, or a flock of sheep, bleating and stumbling, as they were moved from one field to another.

On the way home, we would call in on Nannie Brooks. At her kitchen table we would be given jam on white crusty bread and tea and fairy cakes.

We first heard about the robbery on the news: a mail train. Thieves had stolen over a million pounds in used bank notes from a train near Cheddington. Where is Cheddington we wanted to know? A long way away; at least twenty-five miles or maybe more. And so, life continued much the same as life does in the long summer holidays: games of badminton and hopscotch played beneath the August sun; lines drawn in chalk on the tar bubbled road. And then it wasn't just a million pounds, but much more. More than anyone could imagine. Over two and a half million and the robbers and the money had disappeared without a trace.

'There's something going on at Leatherslade Farm,' the villagers whispered. And the whispers became excited chatter over garden fences, along grassy footpaths and in rutted lanes. And they wanted to know about the tip off, and was it true that the herdsman had seen blacked out windows and land rovers and an army truck? And the herdsman wasn't just a herdsman; he was our friend's dad and they lived just along the road. And we biked to the farm to see what was happening, but we couldn't get close. And men and women, who wouldn't normally go to the Chandos Arms or the Royal Oak, were now sitting with a pint, or a babycham, and talking to reporters from every newspaper, while vans with television cameras lined the grass verges. Camera crews on foot held microphones and carried black cases. Police cars, vans and motorbikes drove around the narrow lanes; and in the skies the beating blades of helicopters as they circled above.

The robbers had gone. Left in a hurry. How much of a hurry? Did they have time to clear up?

'The money,' people asked. 'Did they find the money?' Perhaps it was still hidden; buried beneath a hedge. Had they looked behind the cattle sheds? What about the well? Of course, had anyone thought to drain the well? How many feet deep is a well? There may be bodies. Who knew what they would find in a well that hadn't been used for donkeys years? It had a strange history did Leatherslade. Who knew what they would find when they started poking around.

And of course, there had been sightings. Well, not exactly, not close enough to give a description. And strangers were easy to spot in a village so small, where everyone knew everyone's business. Policemen holding notebooks knocked on doors. Anything suspicious, anything seen, anything heard? And someone who had given a lift to a man in an army jacket and dropped him at the farm entrance couldn't now be quite as sure as he had once been. And the stranger who drank a pint, alone, in the public bar of the Royal Oak, was a man difficult to describe.

The reporters wanted pictures; they wanted action; a story to fill the slots while they waited for news. They hung around the village in droves, waiting for the police to make the next statement, to finish their search, to find new evidence. No news reporter wanted to miss the next big headline.

They said we could be on television. 'You want to be on the news tonight kids?' Of course we did. We didn't need much persuading. Ten year olds don't need reasons. And we were going to get some of the action. Not as onlookers or outsiders, not some sideshow. We were going to hit the big time: the national news.

We straggled down the lane between Emmy's cottage and the Mill House; us leading the way, the camera crew and the reporters following. They wanted a field. They wanted us to look for the money. '

'Find some sticks,' they said, 'pretend you're looking for the money. Look in the grass, in the ditches and in the hedges. See that old shed, climb on top of it. Rummage around a bit, look down the drainpipes.'

We walked back along the lane. 'That's it then kids. See the news at six. Remember which channel.'

We watched. It had a commentary … 'and as the village children continue to search for the money…' and there I was in black and white, looking like a half-wit as I jumped self-consciously from the roof of Ethel's empty chicken shed. An embarrassed smile as I looked directly at the camera.

Three days later it was over. The police had finished. They drove off in police cars with the land rovers and the army truck, the Monopoly board and the Saxa salt pot and anything else that could be used in evidence. No real money, just monopoly. The cars and the camera crews, the motorbikes and the ice cream vans began to leave. The village returned to quiet routine. But it whispered. Was it really possible to get all that money away in such a hurry? And in the lanes and on the verges and at Church after the Sunday service, where the congregation gathered and there was more than usual in the collection plate, the whispers and the rumours did not go away.

'Two and a half tons of money,' they said. 'Two and a half million, and most of that in ten bob notes. A lot to shift in a hurry, wouldn't you say? Wouldn't be surprised if…' If what? And what about the reward. For the tip off. For the herdsman?

The village hall is much the same as it was forty years before: stackable chairs arranged around rectangular tables, each with a centrepiece of flowers, hand tied with red ribbon. An open hatch reveals the recessed canteen where the same huge kettle sits and steams on the back plate of an ancient range.

I am dressed in black.

Among the many faces I see is my Auntie Joan, frail, much older, but still recognisable. We kiss, hug, everything as it ever was.

'I'm sorry about your mum,' she says. 'So sudden.'

'Thank you for coming,' I say. And we talk about the walks along Manor Road, and my mum pushing the old pram beneath the chestnut trees that lined the turnpike and tea with Nannie Brooks. Auntie Joan, not related by blood, but by our shared history. I tell her how I loved those tea-times at her mother's red bungalow. Such a kind, gentle lady.

'She was never the same again,' she says. 'What with the trial and all that business. She looked after the keys to Leatherslade; for the agent. One of the robbers collected the keys from her. She kept them in the kitchen drawer. She never did get over it. Was never the same again'

I try to imagine Nannie Brooks in the Crown Court. Nannie Brooks, who rarely left the village, caught up in a world of gangs and underworld crime. I kiss Auntie Joan good bye. It is the last time I will see her.

And the herdsman and his family, who received the reward, and left the village for fear of reprisals; what became of him? On the wall in the

Chandos Arms, are the school class photographs. His children sit cross legged along with the rest of us. That is the last memory I have of them.

And one day, I will find myself travelling on a train, sitting next to a girl who is also travelling to London. I will tell her why I never entirely believe anything I see on the news.

'Yeah,' she'll say, 'in Belfast when they need to film a riot they throw a handful of pound coins into the street.'

Mary Durndell

Taxi Rides with Daniel

Every morning Mrs Tyson blares the horn,
her immaculate taxi waiting
to take us to school

up the side of the moor past the gorge
where I always look down mesmerized
sure we'd miss the curve,

crash into rocks like teeth at the bottom
where the stream like silver foil tantalized.
I cry out every time,

(but she believes in reincarnation,
fancies being a snake slipping through bracken
shedding skin like responsibility).

Halfway down past the lake
Daniel waits at the end of his lane.
Bare knees touching on sticky leather seats,

my skin needles electric shocks.
As she skids down the hill into Eskdale
I touch Daniel's fingers.

Then one morning he's gone.
Mrs Tyson says he isn't coming back
lips pursed tight in a thin line.

I grieve in the back of her car
as the toy dog nods furiously on the dashboard,
and Mrs T talks about reincarnation.

Cathy Whittaker
Published in Quintet and other Poets, Cinnamon Press.

A Walk in the Woods

I don't remember how I came to be in this place. I had been lying in the warmth where there was brightness and safety and security. I was so tired, but the warmth and the light soaked into my body. The bright sunshine of the afternoon dissolved into the damp darkness of the evening.

I looked about me. The place was familiar but somehow different. I was alone, no longer safe. The grass was wet and the mist all around me. I was cold. I could see trees silhouetted against the darkening sky; a cloudless moon cast a silvery light that shafted between them. I wondered whether I should move towards the trees or just stay where I was.

The shadows were around me; a cold, hostile barrier against the exposed land. I could not make out if they were people or animals but when I really stared they did not move. The stillness scared me. It was too still, wrong, unnatural. I knew this place, a distant memory, but the knowledge held no comfort. Only once had I felt this apprehension, this isolation. I had come over one bright, sunny day. I remember running and running, loving where I was, loving the freedom but then realising I was lost. The cold sweat, panic rising up through me as I glanced from side to side then the relief on seeing a familiar face, knowing I was safe. But this was different. It was dark and grey. The greyness would soon be black. I tried not to make a sound as I moved slowly towards the trees. My legs were leaden, my breathing shallow. I could hear a steady, fast, thudding noise. It took me time to realise this was my heart. I wanted time to rewind, to return to this afternoon, to the warmth and safety of my home. I did not want to be here, the stillness was stifling, there was no life, no sound, nothing to see, just dark, indistinct shapes looming up in the distance.

As I edged into the wood, a shadow moved towards me. It was massive, big and black, it seemed to be folding forward out of the black background. I stopped and stood perfectly still, willing my heart to be quiet. How I wished I too could merge into the background, but I was golden and my gold betrayed me.

'Hey there.' A voice came from the shadow. 'You made it then?'

I wasn't sure what he meant, he did not seem familiar but he acted as if he knew me.

'Yes, I'm here, but I will be going home soon, I'm not really sure why I'm here or how I got here.'

'I've been watching you for some time' he said, his voice was deep but not menacing. 'I am the answer to your questions.'

Barbara Smith

A Basket of Eggs

I'm walking down a sun-baked road with a basket of eggs. The scary thing is, I can't remember who I am or what I'm doing here. Instinctively, I know the eggs are for market, just as I know I don't belong here. Inside me is a big ball of something, fear, or dread. I'm not sure which. It dominates me. I scarcely notice the countryside around me, or the hot sunshine.

I see the village ahead, all pretty white houses, with geraniums and other flowers in pots and window boxes. When I reach it, my feet carry me to the market place. I sit down next to the other people selling things.

Some people smile and nod at me. I nod back, in greeting. I can't understand anything anyone says to me. My heart beats are heavy and fast. My mouth dries. Customers come and I give them eggs, in the paper bags tucked into the basket. When they have questions, or need change, the other vendors help me sort out my money or provide answers for me. They seem familiar with this process.

When all the eggs are sold, I get up and go to the water fountain for a drink. I sit there for a bit wondering what to do next. It preys on my mind that I can't understand what is being said to me. It is as if my thoughts are in another language. I think this might be Greece, but how did I get here? How did I come to be walking down the road with a basket of eggs?

I sit there, trying to remember who I am, how I came to be here, where I live, and chiefly, why I have this constant sense of fear, of panic, even. Why can't I understand the language, when the other people, the vendors and customers, seem to know me?

A car draws up. A man and woman get out. They are obviously rich, probably foreign tourists. They walk around the market place, looking at what is for sale, without buying anything. A couple of the older women, some of my fellow vendors, run off to their houses and return with tablecloths, in which are wrapped some of their work, lace bits and pieces they have worked on during the winter evenings. They start trying to persuade the tourists to buy something. They speak in Greek, I presume.

Watching them, my interest is sparked. The tourists are speaking English! I listen hard, but then I'm not so sure. Some of the words sound English, but others don't. Maybe it is the accent they have, the woman in particular. She does most of the talking. I feel drawn to her. She seems like a motherly person, someone who would be kind to me. I get up and approach them.

The woman sees me and smiles, then puts a hand out and touches my cheek.

'Pretty!' she says.

I recoil as if I have been struck. What does she think I am? A doll or something?

One of the Greek women says something to the tourists, and makes a sign with her hand, referring to me, I know. She is telling them I can't speak, I think. But I can! I've never spoken before, all the time I've been here. But I know I can speak if I want to. Now might be the time to try. I clear my throat, and start with one word.

'English,' I say. I have to make several attempts, but by the third one, the word comes out clearly enough.

The tourist smiles. 'Actually, we're American, not English,' she says, and turns back to the ladies with the lace for sale.

I can scarcely think. Different sensations pound through me: disappointment that she has misunderstood me, understanding that she comes from the land of Mickey Mouse and Hollywood, and that is why her accent is so strange, elation that after countless years I have uttered a word. I have spoken.

'No!' I almost shout. '*I* am English.'

They all turn and stare at me. The Greek women seem amazed, that I can talk. The tourists less so. As ever, the woman is the spokesperson.

'What are you doing here, then?'

'I was stolen, when I was a little girl,' I reply, enunciating each word slowly, deliberately. The words surprise me as much as they clearly surprise her. I don't wish for any misunderstanding. As I say them, I know they are true.

Now the woman is doubtful. 'Are you sure? Where do you live?' I can see her half turning to the Greek women, as if they might be able to tell her.

'*No!*' Once again, my voice rises. '*I can't go back there!*' The terror inside me feels as if it is ready to burst. What will happen if it does? Will I have a heart attack and die? I can feel my breathing, as if I have been running a very long distance.

Help comes from an unlikely quarter. The male tourist touches me lightly on the arm. 'It's all right,' he says. 'No-one is going to hurt you. Come and sit down.' He leads me over to the water fountain, where he urges me to sit and have a drink of water. I do, and presently feel better. I look around. Both tourists are gazing at me curiously. The Greek ladies and several more Greek men are watching me closely.

The American man seems inclined to take control now. 'Were you really stolen from your family when you were small?' he asks.

I nod.

'What is your name?' he asks.

'I can't remember.'

'Really?'

'I might be able to remember, but something has frightened me so much that I can't remember anything.'

'Trauma,' cuts in the American woman.

The man nods and I look from one to the other, wondering what the word means, and if it is a way of saying they think I'm a liar.

'Can you tell me what frightened you?' the man continues.

I begin to shake my head, then things begin popping into my mind. 'Paolo,' I say. I feel faint at the sound of his name. 'The old lady who looked after me, I had to call her mother, only I never did, she died. She used to protect me from him. He is her son. She was buried yesterday.' Suddenly I give a sob and rub tears away from my eyes. 'He tries to . . . touch me . . . there,' I touch my breasts briefly, 'and there.' I put my hands down to my crotch. 'I'm . . . I'm frightened of him. I can't go back there.'

'Can't the police help?' the American woman asks.

'Huh. They'd just send me back to him.' I mumble my words. I am aware of the Greek people gathering closer.

'If you're sure about being English, you need to go the British Embassy in Athens,' her husband says. We both look at him.

'But we just came from Athens, honey,' the wife says.

'We'll be going back in a week or so. She can come along with us until then, can't she?' The couple look at each other. An unspoken agreement is struck.

I leave the village, driving in a motor car for the first time, and safe for the first time in a long time, thanks to my new American friends.

'What do you think, Wilbur? She'd look kinda cute in this, wouldn't she?'

Mrs Vanderbilt is engaged in her favourite activity, buying me clothes. At first, I expected Mr Vanderbilt to object, to say she is spending far too much money on me. But he never does, and after a while I realise that really, money is no object for them. Making Mrs Vanderbilt happy is high on his list of priorities, however, and if that means kitting me out in all manner of all-American style dresses, hot pants, bikinis, etc, then so be it. Half the garments I am sure I will never be able to bring myself to wear.

I am learning a bit more about the world. Mrs Vanderbilt seems to see it as part of her duty to inform me who the President of the United States is, although she is a bit less sure about the Prime Minister of Great Britain. She tells me Queen Elizabeth is still on the throne. I feel quite pleased that I can remember that detail from when I was a child.

She is scandalised when I tell her I never went to school in Greece. Of course, the old lady who stole me, hid me away from the authorities. Then there was my dumbness. I tell them how I had been almost like a vegetable when they let me out of the car boot.

'Trauma,' says Mrs Vanderbilt, again.

I explain that at first I couldn't talk or do anything. Then I decided not to talk, as a sort of silent protest against my captivity.

'Did those Greek women in the village tell you I couldn't talk?' I ask. 'They made a sort of sign.' I demonstrate the sign.

'Er, no, dear.' Mrs Vanderbilt looks embarrassed. 'They were telling me you were . . . a bit slow witted.'

Indignation grows inside me. But what can I do? Just show my new friends I'm not in the least slow witted.

Now the danger from Paulo has receded, the feeling of fear inside me has shrunk to manageable proportions. I remember things, like Greek words. In fact, I can translate quite a lot of things for my new friends. Spoken things, that is, because I never learnt to read or write in Greek. And, of course, my English education stopped when I was seven years old.

After a week of driving along bumpy Greek roads and staying in funny little hotels, we arrive in Athens. After one night in a big, posh hotel, we go the British Embassy. I feel embarrassed that no matter how hard I try, I can't remember my English name. My Greek name is Maria. It is the name the Vanderbilts call me by. I hate it.

The man at the Embassy listens to my story. I have no idea how old I am, but the Vanderbilts think I might be about seventeen. On the day I walked down the road with the basket of eggs, it was as if a switch had flicked in my brain, and my memory of the past ten years had gone.

The man gets out a file of children reported missing in Greece, turns the pages, pauses, looks at me, says: 'Isabel?' and I say: 'Yes'. I feel weak. A big hollow space inside me is filling up with faces, a man and woman, my parents, my sister, our house in England, my school and school friends.

He holds up a photo. I recognise it. It is my own face, a little girl with fair hair, although my hair is mid-brown now. It is as easy as that. Suddenly, I have an identity, a past, a family.

He wants to know where I've been for the last ten years. I explain as best as I can. An old woman, whose only daughter had died when she was about seven, her adult son who resolved to find a replacement for her, and stole a little English girl who wandered too far from the tourist beaches. I don't tell him about the repeated sexual assaults down through the years, which increase when the old lady dies, somehow causing the new panic attack that left me walking along a road with a basket of eggs and no memory.

Phone calls are made. A man and two women arrive in Athens. The older woman rushes forward to embrace me. I let her, not welcoming the human contact, but realising this is important for her. Over her bowed head, I am looking at the younger woman, making eye contact with my older sister, for the first time in ten years.

As I gaze at her the world around me dissolves and I stand once more on a lonely beach, a long way from the hotel. The old Greek lady and the younger Greek man, her son, stand before me. The old lady looks at me, nodding, talking to me, in Greek; offering me some Greek sweetmeat, which I look at suspiciously. Then my sister speaking to the Greek man, an exchange of money, and my sister turning and running back towards the hotel. I was dragged, kicking and screaming, in the opposite direction. A blanket was wrapped around me and I was thrust into the boot of an old, rusty car. We drove many miles, to my new life as the 'daughter' of an old Greek peasant woman, who could not get over the death of her only daughter, many years before.

My mother is blowing her nose, speaking to me. The image of the beach slips away. Looking into my face, she says. 'Isabel. I never thought I'd see you again.' Another burst of tears.

My father pats her on the back, smiling at me, detaching her from my shoulder, and on to his own.

'It's good to have you back, Izzy.' I remember, he always called me 'Izzy'. 'Do you remember your sister Cassandra? Of course you do.' He is reaching for her hand, drawing her forward to greet me.

I look into my sister's eyes. Fear and pleading. Pleading with me not to tell. 'Don't tell, Izzy.' It was what she always said when she did something naughty. Fear! Fear that I will give her away. Fear that I will tell everyone, our parents, others, that she sold me for five hundred drachmas.

'Five hundred drachmas,' I murmur, looking straight at her.

'What was that?' asks my father.

'I said, of course I remember. How could I forget? Hello, Cassy. It's good to see you again, after all these years.'

I managed it. The words haven't stuck in my throat. It costs me a lot, but after what my parents have suffered for the last ten years, how can I inflict even more pain on them? And I can see that she has suffered too, with the enormity of what she had done, all those years ago. She is still suffering, now. She is on a spit, roasting on the fire of her jealousy and lies and deceit. And I can give that spit a little turn whenever I want.

Five hundred drachmas, Cassy. Five hundred drachmas.

Senga Hawker

This Summer

Scenting heavy perfumed pine this summer,
grapes taken straight from vine this summer.

Walking ancient hedge-bound rights of way,
guided by the acorn sign this summer.

Chasing butterflies, champagne flutes in hand,
drinking ice cool vintage wine this summer.

Hanging baskets draped on white brick walls,
sweet peas growing in a line this summer.

Glimpsing cloud-cradled moon and evening stars,
sensing heavenly design this summer.

Touching sun warmed stones and gentle grass,
holding hands and feeling fine this summer.

The greater gift for Paul than all of these,
knowing, Mary, you are mine this summer.

Paul Budd

Mothers and Daughters, Daughters and Mothers.

'I hate you!' She slams the door and, deliberately stamping her feet heavily on the stairs, retreats to her bedroom. Another door slam, sufficient this time to dislodge a poster from the wall; it peels away from its sellotape and floats to the floor. She marches across the room to stand in front of the mirror. Hands on hips, she turns her head one way and then the other. Her tiny mini skirt clings to her thighs. She stamps her feet again, her black boots making a satisfying thud on the floor. She sticks a frustrated tongue out at her reflection and defiantly turns the knob on her transistor to its highest setting. She fluffs up her back-combed hair and re-applies her white lipstick. I look good, she thinks, and I'm going out like this, whatever she says.

﹒﹒﹒﹒﹒﹒﹒﹒﹒﹒﹒﹒﹒﹒﹒﹒﹒﹒﹒﹒﹒﹒﹒﹒﹒﹒﹒﹒

You stand in the kitchen, another house, another time, another you. You shrink slightly under the onslaught from the young girl standing in front of you, her over-bright eyes challenging and defiant. 'You don't understand,' she shouts. 'You're stuck in the dark ages'. You start to speak but she's never going to listen. She slings her bag over her shoulder and flicks back her long blonde hair as she turns to leave. 'Everyone else is allowed out till twelve. I can look after myself'. She pauses by the door. 'Just think yourself lucky that I don't do drugs'. She comes back to grab her mobile and a packet of cigarettes from the work surface. You try to ignore the cigarettes, just reassured that she takes her phone. 'Is it charged?' you ask automatically. 'For God's sake Mum, leave it will you.' She pulls open the door and leaves with no goodbye. You watch from the window as she swings away down the path and out onto the street.

﹒﹒﹒﹒﹒﹒﹒﹒﹒﹒﹒﹒﹒﹒﹒﹒﹒﹒﹒﹒﹒﹒﹒﹒﹒﹒﹒﹒

Now here I am sitting by a bed, in the night-time quiet of a darkened room. The gentle glow of a bedside lamp lights quilted bedcovers which hardly move; the sound of laboured breathing is the only evidence of its occupant. The inevitable trappings of illness spoil the room: a row of medicine bottles are lined up along the delicate French dressing table, an ugly commode squats in the corner by the polished mahogany chest. Her pretty embroidered cushions have been discarded on the bedside chair and are joined now by piles of crisp white surgical packs. Her familiar scent of Channel No 5 is only just discernible through the sad smell of the dying. I carefully lift her hand, my fingers stroke the wrinkled skin.

I turn slightly at the quiet creak of an opening door. A young woman steps into the room and silently offers me a cup of tea. Her long blonde hair brushes my cheek as she reaches across to place it on the bedside table. She kneels down on the floor beside my chair, one hand on the bedcover, one hand seeking mine. We sit quietly together holding hands and watching the peaceful, sleeping face. I smile and gently stroke the hair from my Mother's face. 'She's still beautiful' I whisper.

Erica Guise

Eleven Lords a Leaping

When Julia arrived at the outer office of the Home Secretary, the principal private secretary greeted her and took her through at once.

'Lady Clarke, Home Secretary', the assistant said, closing the door behind him as he withdrew.

George McGinty walked around his desk to greet her.

'Good Morning, Julia – thank you very much for coming at such short notice.'

'Good Morning, George – I hope you're well'.

'Yes, quite well, Julia - and you?'

'I'm fine, thank you.'

The pleasantries over, George indicated a seat in front of his desk. Julia sat down.

'Right, I need to tell you what this is about.'

He brought his chair round to sit across from her. 'I'll get to the point straight away' he said as he sat down.

'Yesterday, the Prime Minister told me that he's very keen on setting up a sporting fixture between the Lords and the Commons which, he hopes, might become an annual event.'

'Did he have anything particular in mind?' Julia asked wondering what this had to do with her.

'Well, his suggestion was a cricket match. As you know it's a game he's very fond of. Probably sometime in June, before the recess. He asked if I would be willing to take charge of organising it.'

George looked at her for a moment.

'That's where you come in Julia.'

'Me? Now, George… where are you heading with this?'

He banged his hand on the desk and gave her a beaming smile

'Right, Julia! This is my plan. As a former Olympic athlete turned politician turned Baroness Clarke of Tything and my Junior Minister I want *you* to look after the Lords' team and I will do the same for the Commons.'

Julia looked at her boss as if he'd taken leave of his senses.

'George, thank you for offering but I have to decline. I've never been to a cricket match in my life! I don't know what the rules are, how many players take part, what you have to do to win …'

'Come on, Julia, where's that Olympian spirit I've heard so much about?'

'I was an *athlete*, George, not a cricketer! This would be like asking me to take out somebody's appendix without ever having trained as a surgeon!'

The Home Secretary threw his head back laughing so hard that Julia wondered if she'd missed her vocation as a professional comedian.

'You don't have to *play* the game' George said. 'You just need to be the strategist behind it. There will be so many members of the Lords wanting to take part that the only problem you'll have is picking the team – and you can always get someone to help you with that.'

Julia was about to argue this further when George's phone rang. She glanced down at her watch; she was going to be late for another appointment. She gestured that she needed to leave and left George to his phone call. Walking back down the corridor Julia realised it was already too late to get out of this. She was saddled with something she neither wanted nor needed.

It was now 'game on'.

Over the next few days, posters were put up in Members' dining rooms, libraries and even the terraces. Those interested in participating were asked to add their names. At least twenty Members of the House of Commons registered. Julia was not so fortunate. From the upper chamber, only five Noble Lords had stepped forward to face the Commons challenge.

With the two-week deadline for signing up expiring later that day, Julia knew that unless more people made themselves available the match wouldn't be going ahead.

Only a short time ago, she'd have been relieved beyond words that she'd been let off the hook but now she was all fired up and ready to go.

In between Bills, Sittings and Meetings she'd spent her time learning about this game, this cricket. She now knew everything there was to know about it; overs, runs, silly mid offs, lbws, umpires, bowlers, wicketkeepers and every other aspect of this weird and wonderful sporting eccentricity. The truth was, by now, she couldn't wait to pick her team and beat the living daylights out of the Commons!

But, the disappointing reality was she had only five players. She was about to email the Home Secretary and give him the bad news when the 'Olympian spirit' George had referred to, welled up inside her.

'Right Julia.' She told herself. 'Carpe Diem!'

Reaching for the Register of Members, she started to flick through. After a few minutes, she had a random list of names in front of her. She took a couple of deep breaths and reached for the phone, punching in the first number.

'Hello, Peter! How's it all going? Good! Good to hear'

Lord Peter Fairfax had a reputation for talking, often about himself! In the circumstances, Julia decided to indulge him. When he paused for breath, she got in before he started up again.

'Peter, another reason for my call is that I assume you hadn't realised that today's the closing date for registering for the Lords' Cricket team. I must tell you that I'm banking on you to lead the rout. I have you earmarked as a potential captain …. Yes, yes, I rather suspected you might have captained the first eleven at Eton – that doesn't surprise me at all!'

Julia wriggled – sycophancy didn't come easy to her but she had chosen her subject well.

'Excellent, Peter; you will be an indispensable member of the squad. Practice nets tomorrow at St John's Park, 10.30? … Good! See you then, Bye!'

'One down, five to go' she said, speaking out loud.

The next couple of hours didn't go quite so well. The two women members she tried to persuade were adamant, they couldn't play. Lord Featherstone also refused but then agreed to take part if he could be opening batsman.

She struck it lucky a little later. After popping out to get a coffee she bumped into two, relatively new, peers and managed to steer the conversation around to cricket. It didn't take too long to persuade them to join the Lords' team. It was unfortunate they didn't mention that neither of them had ever played cricket before!

She raced through the rest of the list. Some members weren't answering. She suspected they knew why she was ringing and were hiding in cupboards and under tables. Finally, she spoke to Bill Bell, whom everyone knew as Lord Ding Dong, and made her case so strongly he had no choice but to say 'yes'. She was surprised and pleased when Bill offered to speak to another peer, Tom Miller, whom he said had played cricket in his youth.

She breathed a sigh of relief. At last they had a team.

The next few weeks were hectic. Every morning before the Lords sat, this disparate group from the Upper Chamber came together on St John's Park and worked together as they would never have done in the House. Camaraderie, team spirit, brotherly love (well, perhaps that was going a bit too far) became the order of the day with Julia, as coach and John Duxbury as her number two.

They bowled, batted and fielded until their limbs ached. The two absolute beginners took to it like ducks to water and even those who had been more resistant at the beginning put their hearts and souls into it. There was some concern about Lord Spicer, who at eighty-one couldn't do very much by way of running between the wickets. With as much tact as she could muster, Julia suggested that he came in at number eleven in the hope he might not need to bat. He agreed, saying something like he would prefer playing in that position then he could 'finish 'em off!'

The great day dawned and St John's Park had never seen anything like it. The sun was shining, birds were singing and the two teams, resplendent in their 'whites' had come together to have their photograph taken with the Prime Minister, who had donated the shield which would be presented to the winning team at the end of the game.

There was a magnificent crowd of at least 30 people and everyone settled down to enjoy a splendid day's play.

It had been agreed to restrict each innings to twenty overs. The Commons won the toss and chose to bat. The two Openers - the Home Secretary and the Chancellor of the Exchequer - walked out on to the pitch to great applause from their supporters. There was an immediate success for the Lords as the Chancellor was clean bowled first ball. He stood there for a moment or two, shocked and bemused, looking towards the umpire in the vain hope he would find something wrong with the bowler's action. The umpire was having none of it and indicated the Chancellor had to go. Looking altogether dejected, he walked off the field, the way he'd come.

The next batsman was Clive Abbot, a Liberal Democrat backbencher, and now, the Commons' crowd got behind their team. Even Julia had to admit that what followed afterwards was nothing short of impressive. George and Clive coped with everything bowled at them: bouncers, in swingers, googlies. It didn't matter whether they faced slow, fast, medium or spin or who was brought on to deliver them, at the end of the twenty overs they were still there and the score was a magnificent eighty-three for one. They received a standing ovation from partisan and opposition supporters alike and as they left the field they raised their bats above their heads in acknowledgment.

Julia had very mixed feelings at this point. Her intrinsic sense of fair play respected the Commons' performance; but, her competitive streak screamed out in frustration. She knew they'd be lucky to make thirty runs let alone half the Commons' score.

They would be mincemeat as soon as their opponents warmed up.

As promised, Lord Featherstone led out as opening batsman accompanied by Lord Fairfax as Captain.

'Please let then get at least one run each,' she said to her assistant coach.

Featherstone scored five and Fairfax seven. However, as the batsmen came and went and the score crept upwards at a very slow pace, and still woefully short of the thirty she had hoped for, Julia began to feel very despondent. They were near the tail enders and Lord Spicer was now fast asleep! So much for their number eleven.

She spoke to the umpire.

'Can we send out one of the other batsmen again, please? Lord Spicer may not be able to play'.

'No!' said the umpire, without equivocation, 'That's not allowed, Lady Clarke. I'm surprised at you!'

Julia walked away feeling chastened as well as depressed.

They passed the thirty mark at the end of the sixteenth over, coinciding with their ninth wicket being caught behind for eight. There was nothing for it, they would have to concede the game or wake up Lord Spicer.

Julia was amazed to see him on his feet already, padded up and pulling on an ancient cap that looked as if it had seen much better days.

As he walked out, using his bat as a walking stick, Lord Spicer was heard to say, non-too sotto voce, 'Bugger this for a game of cricket!'

Julia watched as he reached the wicket.

'I wonder if he still has it in him.' Julia realised it was the Prime Minister standing next to her.

'Sorry, Prime Minister, we had no choice but to send him out – he really *did* want to play, you know'

'I should think he did' said the Prime Minister 'He was still going strong when I was a lad and he was well into his forties by then. He inspired me as he did many other boys into playing cricket; he was a shining example of sportsmanship and fair play.'

Just at that moment a cheer went up. Julia had missed what had happened out on the field. She glanced back to see the umpire indicating 'four', and then saw Lord Spicer preparing himself for another delivery.

The next ball came hurtling down the wicket and Lord Spicer leant into it and hit it across the ground for another boundary. Eight runs already in the over!

He prodded the ground in front of him, received the next delivery with complete disdain, and hit it for six!

Julia, by this time, was standing there open-mouthed.

'Prime Minister' she said, 'How do you know Lord Spicer?'

'Jimmy Spicer played for Lancashire and England in the 1950s and early 60s. He was the most marvellous ambassador for the game: a true sportsman and a great player'

'He never said a word about his past. I had no idea' said Julia 'I'm completely bowled over – if I can say that, of course!'

They stood watching this man play with the determination, skill and the energy of someone half his age.

It was the Commons' turn now to bring on the heavyweights. Despite this, he survived everything they threw at him and, because he didn't run between the wickets, he and the other batsman had to rely solely on his boundaries to build up the score. And build it up he did!

When they got to seventy-five, Julia couldn't watch anymore. The excitement was just too much. The crowd was on its feet.

'Go on, Jimmy' yelled someone 'Nearly there!'

Keeping his head down and not allowing anybody to distract him, Lord Spicer hit another six.

Julia crossed her fingers whispering 'eighty-one, just one more boundary'

Disaster struck with the next ball! He was clean bowled. The whole crowd fell silent.

Everyone looked at the umpire who was holding an arm outstretched indicating that the delivery was 'a no ball.' Lord Spicer was not out!

The bowler's expression said it all as he walked back rubbing the ball so vigorously he almost made a hole in his new white trousers.

The crowd waited. The bowler started to run and the delivery came fast and furious. Jimmy Spicer, former county cricketer, former England batsman, received it as one would a welcome gift from a friend, collecting it in the centre of his bat and smacking it away firmly and decisively for four.

The whole park erupted. What a win!

The two batsmen walked off the field to cheers and applause from everyone.

Julia walked over to Lord Spicer.

'Why didn't you tell me?' she said.

'Well, it was a long time ago and there was no guarantee I could come up with the goods'

Julia then realised what the Prime Minster had meant earlier. This was a very modest, unassuming man who had played for his county and country in a very different era when praise and adulation was given but in a much more measured way. He was right in his assessment of a true sportsman.

It was time for the presentation of the shield and they all milled around, waiting for the Prime Minister to speak.

'This has been a truly memorable game of cricket between two very good teams. Each of you played well but it would be remiss of me not to single out two or three players who were exceptional and I think you know who they are.'

The Prime Minister went on to summarise the first innings and the remarkable partnership between George and Clive. He then moved on to the second innings and was the soul of discretion in describing the form of most of the team until, at length, he came to J. Spicer.

'When I was a boy, he was an inspiration to us all. He was my hero. Today he played as if the intervening years had never taken place. It has been my pleasure and privilege to be here and see such a great man show us all how it should be done. And so, without further ado, I have no hesitation in naming my man of the match: Lord Spicer!'

A great roar went up and every single person clapped and saluted a living legend.

'And now, I would like to invite Lord Featherstone, as Captain of the winning team to come forward and collect the 'Parliamentary Cricket Shield'. I hope this will be the first of many games between the Lords and the Commons and that some of you will come back next year to continue the fight'

Julia saw Lord Featherstone hesitate and say something to Lord Spicer. He was asking Jimmy to collect the shield. The chivalrous gesture wasn't lost on anyone.

Lord Spicer walked with dignity and pride towards the Prime Minister.

As he was handed the shield, everyone, whether Lords or Commons supporters, clapped with genuine admiration.

The Prime Minister held up his hand and indicated that he had something else to say.

'Colleagues, I would like to bring one last thing to your attention. My hope is that you will join with me in celebrating and acknowledging something quite remarkable. I am referring to the fact that we have here before us, even though there are still six months to go until Christmas, none other than …'

He turned and extended his arm towards the triumphant team.

'The original…. the authentic, 'Eleven Lords a Leaping!'

And with these words, the Lords did indeed, almost as one, begin to leap around without regard for health, safety, decorum or convention. Julia knew there would be stiff joints in the morning but, just for today, no-one cared.

It was a most famous victory, one that she and rest of them would most likely never forget for the rest of their lives.

Margaret Ward

Chain Link

I have long been acquainted with the clock
I have wound and rewound its long brass chain
I have grown to love that gleaming clock

I once listened to its beat with pain.
In time I learned to hear my mother's voice
Tell my eager ears the rhythmic refrain

Until I absorbed the saga, began to rejoice
To find comfort in the family story
In the steady mellow beating noise

Its ticking voice dictates the order as ordained
Great grandmother grandma mother daughter
The dues of family at each stage sustained

But I know that one day in the future
This chain linked bond through time will rupture.

Hazel Cross
After 'Acquainted with the Night' by Robert Frost.
Published in The Cannon's Mouth, Cannon Poets Quarterly, December 2013

The Ballad of Hannah Twinnoy

To Malmesbury the circus came,
three hundred years ago.
A caravan of many acts,
menagerie in tow.

The animals had been traded
on dark and distant shores.
From Africa and India,
no licences or laws.

Excited townsfolk gathered round
to witness the display,
whilst showmen searched beside the church
for somewhere they could stay.

'They can't graze here,' the folk complained,
'For this is sacred land.
They're better by the White Lion Inn,
the pasture there is grand.'

The wagons trundled up the hill
along the Gloucester Road.
They found the inn and settled in,
then started to unload.

They tied the tiger in the yard
and warned the gazing throng,
'A fiercer beast you'll never meet,
near him you'll not live long.'

The barmaid's name was Hannah,
a migrant to the town,
a girl of single-mindedness,
a rebel and a clown.

The tiger's claws and awesome roars
for Hannah held no fear.
She teased the cat, believing that
she'd never get too near.

'You'll come to grief,' the keeper warned,
'I've told you, let him be.
A tiger's not the kind of beast
that plays with you or me.'

But Hannah grew more confident,
no warnings she'd accept.
With snapping jaws and pouncing paws
the angry tiger leapt.

Around the town of Malmesbury
church bells were heard to ring,
'the tiger at the Lion Inn
has done a dreadful thing.'

From Gloucester Road to Gloucester Street
then through the Abbey gate,
a humble barmaid laid to rest
beside the good and great.

Of Hannah Twinnoy's circumstance
a mystery remains.
Who paid the poet, carved the stone,
and who would take such pains?

So, did the poet's words convey
a message, sad, wherein,
'In bloom of life,'* did surely mean
an unborn child within?

Hannah Twinnoy died on the twenty-third of October 1703 aged thirty-three. She is believed to be the first person in Great Britain to be killed by a tiger. She was buried at Malmesbury Abbey. The inscription on her gravestone reads:

*In bloom of life
She's snatch'd from hence
She had not room
To make defence;
For Tyger fierce
Took Life away.
And here she lies
In a bed of Clay,
Until the Resurrection Day

Mary Durndell

The Airport Café

'Thanks for the lift, Mum. It's OK, you don't need to come in with me,' her daughter said through the open car window.

'No, I want to Francesca. Besides, I need a coffee before starting back. I'll just park and see you at the coffee shop near the check in desks,' Marietta said.

'OK.' Francesca slammed the car boot shut, slung her bag over one shoulder and wheeled her suitcase into the airport terminal. Five minutes later Marietta found her daughter. Francesca was sitting at a small table in the coffee shop with two lattés. She was speaking to someone on her phone, but put it away as Marietta approached.

'Did you want anything to eat?' Francesca asked.

'No, I'm fine thanks. And thanks for getting the coffees. That's great.' Marietta sat down and took a sip. 'Actually, I've got something to tell you.'

'Really? Don't tell me you and Dad are divorcing at long last! I've got something to tell you too.'

'Have you? What is it? You're not pregnant, are you?'

'Mum! I'm not entirely stupid, you know. I *am* on the *pill*.'

'Are you? Since when?'

'Oh, I don't know. About two years.'

'But you've only just turned eighteen!'

Her daughter shrugged.

Marietta sighed. 'What is it then?' she asked.

Francesca sipped her coffee. 'I'm not going to boring old Marie-Claire's.'

'Poor Marie-Claire. I thought you'd outgrown her when she came to England last year. I wish you'd told me before we came all the way here!'

'I'm going somewhere else instead. Spain.'

'Spain! Who with? I suppose you've got a boyfriend. Really, Francesca. You might have told me. I'm not an ogre, am I? It's not what's-his-name with the acne, is it?'

'Spotty Billy? Have a heart, Mum.' A little smile played about her mouth. 'Actually, he's an older man.'

'Goodness! I hope you know what you're doing.' She looked at Francesca. It was as if she had never seen her before. Yes, the ugly (well, slightly over-weight) duckling had turned into a graceful, elegant swan. Or in other words, she'd grown up. 'After all, you are only just eighteen.'

'Oh, Mum!' Francesca sighed elaborately. 'Anyway, what's your news? What were you going to tell me?'

Marietta hesitated slightly. 'You were right. When you get back, I won't be here. I'm leaving your father.'

'Gosh. Er, what about me? I mean, where will you be?'

'Remember when Granny died, I inherited her house?'

'You're not going to live in that dump, are you? Anyway, I thought you'd sold it.'

'I did. I bought a nice flat instead. I don't know why Granny didn't think of doing that years ago. But anyway, I was going to suggest you stay with your father. I, er, may have a friend living with me.'

'A friend! A boyfriend, you mean? Mum, at your age, that is *gross*!'

'No, it's not! How old do you think I am?'

'Sorry, sorry. You can do as you want, of course. You haven't got yourself a toy-boy, have you?'

'No, I have not! He may be *slightly* younger than me, but there's not really much in it. We haven't spoken about it yet, so it may not happen.'

'Oh well. I'll stick with Dad, I suppose. Unless . . . Well, I'd better stick with Dad.'

They both drank their coffee. Marietta saw the tall, handsome man approaching their table before her daughter. He could easily have been mistaken for George Clooney, she thought, experiencing that little flutter of the heart that she always felt when she saw him. He gave that crooked little smile when he caught her eye.

'James! What are you doing here?' Marietta's eyes took in the casual, holiday type clothes, the suitcase he was towing.

'Hello, Marietta. I'm just off on holiday, actually. Two weeks in sunny Spain. Ready Babe?'

'Sure am, James.' Francesca rose from her seat in one easy, fluid movement. 'Thanks for the lift, Mum. Catch up with you soon!' She bent down and gave Marietta a quick peck on the cheek. Marietta was speechless. She watched her daughter turn and weave her way through the tables, her arm tucked proprietarily through her boyfriend's.

Senga Hawker

Promises

Everyone watches, everyone waits.
Lovers turn to face each other
she in striking wine-coloured silk
he in elegant slate-grey wool.
Each in turn makes a solemn promise
eyes alight with glowing love.

A solemn moment caught in time.

Scents mingle, a pot-pourri
of heady subtle fragrances.
Colours splash across the canvas
crimsons, emeralds, fuchsias, golds
in stark contrast to the quiet greys
the muted hues of suited men.

A vivid picture framed in time.

Vows made, signatures witnessed
hands clasped, congratulations voiced
warm smooth cheeks are lightly kissed
butterfly touches, expressions of joy.
Soft music plays then swells in triumph
as guests applaud the happy pair.

A precious moment locked in time.

Hazel Cross

What's Going to Keep Her Out of Heaven Tonight?

He thinks I don't know what's happening but something is going on. He seems different somehow. He's always dressed up now, well-groomed all of the time. He has a spring in his step and a light in his eye. He says he goes to the park most lunchtimes, to wind down, to clear his head, enjoy the fresh air rather than the stale, recycled, used air of the office. But this time, when he called, he sounded different too. He told me he wouldn't be coming back tonight, that he'd be staying at work really late, so he was going to book in overnight at the hotel next door. It was not to disturb me, he said, but that's not true. Of course, it does, I know. I wanted to say something, to let him know I knew what he was doing, but I feel so scared. Do I really want to know for sure?

This has never happened before, which makes this so significant, more serious. I have never considered losing him, of him going and never coming back. Now it seems it could really happen. I open a bottle of wine. The Sancerre that he raves about. I must start thinking about what life would be like without him. I don't want to be a victim: the silly wife stuck at home, the last to know. I don't want to be devastated and lonely. At the same time, I don't want him staying just because he feels sorry for me or worse because he realises he can't afford to leave.

That happened to a friend of mine. Her husband had always been discontented, obviously unhappy. They just weren't suited. They never really liked each other, almost despising one another. Then he met someone else. He reckoned she was the love of his life. They met at work. She was also in an unsatisfactory and unfulfilling partnership. They agreed that they would announce their relationship and leave their respective partners. At the time, it was clear that this was doomed to failure. The whole process sounded too business like. Anyway, they went ahead, but all too quickly it fizzled out. She wanted to continue. He decided that he couldn't afford to divorce my friend, so he went back to her. She tried to pretend that everything was fine, that nothing had happened, but I thought she was just fooling herself. I was never fooled. They split up again years later. This time it was her decision. For all those years that they were together, he was bitterly unhappy, it was far too high a price to pay. He's with his 'love'. Why she waited, God only knows, but she did. Maybe they're happy. My friend sat pretty in those wilderness years, biding her time. She saved and squirreled away money, hiding inheritances so that when she decided to call a halt on the so called marriage she came out considerably better off. I guess she did actually have the last laugh. I hear he's drinking heavily again and spending hours in the pub alone.

I thought we were different to them. I know we might be cooling off, drifting apart, not bothering to listen to each other, not taking an interest, a real interest I mean, in what we were doing. Just not been bothered, not caring, but I didn't ever think it would come to this.

Now I wait and I plan, I hope he is going to change his mind, to come back tonight. He won't though, so I know that when I drive to that office block and find them, only one of us will be driving away. This wine tastes sour but I'll finish it before I go.

Barbara Smith

If Only We'd Stayed at Home that Day

We are standing in arrivals, hardly speaking. I check and re-check the arrivals board. Nothing yet. I push up my sleeves and squint quickly at my watch. We are ridiculously early; the plane hasn't even left Cairo yet. Sarah holds her mobile carefully in her hand. They've promised to ring her as soon as there is any news.

Neither of us slept much last night. I heard Sarah get up before it was light and then the ping of the computer as she checked and re-checked the details. By seven I could stand it no longer. Stiff with tension, I swung my legs out of the bed and grabbed some clothes from the chair.

'Cup of tea love?' I asked.

'Thanks Mum.' She pushed her hair from her face and stood up from the desk. 'It's all still the same,' she added.

I nodded. 'That's good'. There was nothing else to say, we'd said it all before. I looked at the dark circles under her eyes and wanted to say 'I am **so** sorry'. But I've said it too many times.

For the next hour, we tried to busy ourselves around the flat, tipping away half-drunk cups of tea, washing the mugs; only to start the cycle all over again five minutes later.

I stood in the doorway and watched as Sarah went again into Matilda's room. The smell of new paint and fresh linen lingered in the air. 'Perhaps I should have left it as it was,' she murmured.

'It looks lovely,' I said from the doorway. The walls were a trendy pale mauve with a sophisticated bed cover and curtains to match. A television sat on the chest at the bottom of the bed and a vase of flowers on the bedside table. 'She'll love it,' I said, hoping that my tone was reassuring. A battered teddy and a fairy mobile were the only reminders of the room as I remembered it: when fairy wallpaper covered the walls, a pink princess bedspread over the bed, and toys littered across the floor. A little girl's room where I had read bedtime stories to my darling Tilda, her inky black hair, inherited from her Father, spread over the pillow and her dark lashes hovering over her cheeks as she drifted off to sleep.

Sarah told me endlessly that it was not my fault, that she didn't blame me – but I blamed myself. Every night over the past seven years I've thought of her – if only we'd stayed at home that day, made cakes, done some painting, anything but go to the fête.

We went back into the sitting room, turned on the television, but we weren't watching it, both of us glancing continually at the bright silver clock on the wall above the sofa. I pretended not to watch as Sarah went back to the computer to check again. If only we'd stayed at home that day. It had seemed such a perfect opportunity. The village shop had been showing posters about the fête for days before – just a traditional village fête my neighbours had said: Punch and Judy, slides, balloons that sort of thing, nothing grand, just for the villagers'. I'd not long moved into the village but it sounded safe and I phoned Sarah that night, managing to convince her that it would do Matilda good. Matilda had been rather withdrawn and quiet since her parents' separation. I guessed she was probably missing her friends at nursery school.

It had been one of those rare things: a beautiful English summer's day. The picture book type with a bright sun and big blue skies with just the occasional fluffy white cloud. I'd suggested that we could do some painting when we got home. Matilda's plump hand had been warm in mine. I'd held it tightly as we crossed the green towards the playing fields. She'd trotted trustingly beside me as we walked around the stalls, sat on my knee as we'd watched Mr Punch swing his newspaper at Judy, laughed when the dog ran off with the sausages and hidden her face in my neck when Mr Plod appeared. We'd watched the clown, bought a balloon in the shape of a dog. She had giggled happily when I tickled her nose with its tail.

We heard the ice cream van as it came down the lane. We heard its tune as it turned onto the green. We heard it as it bumped down the track and through the field gate. By the time it pulled onto the playing field, Matilda was already pulling at my hand. 'Ice cream Granny, ice cream'.
My purse must have been deep in my bag and as I passed the cone to Matilda, I reached for it. As I searched for my purse - I let go of her hand. I let go of my darling Tilda's hand.

The policewoman passed me a tissue when I read through my statement, the words blurring through my tears.
'It was all so quick,' I said. 'She must have been standing right behind me. She grabbed Matilda and ran through the gate towards the road. I chased after them, shouting. In seconds, they were in the car and gone. Matilda's ice cream was trampled in the grass.'

The policewoman patted my hand. 'Take your time. Try to remember everything that happened. Did you see who was driving?' she asked.

I had known instantly who it was but I stuttered over a reply, knowing I must only say what I had actually seen. 'I could just see the back of his head, a man with dark black hair,' I said.

She told me not to worry, that they'd find her, that most missing children are returned to their homes within twenty-four hours. But Sarah and I soon found out that 'most' did not mean all.

And so, I re-told my statement again and again: to another policeman, to the man from Interpol, and, as the days went endlessly on, to the solicitor, to the Home Office, to the MP, to a private detective, to the Home Office again. Every time I cried. Sometimes I said it in my head, sometimes out loud, 'If only we'd stayed at home that day.' But 'if only' didn't change the ending. The agonising days dragged on into weeks, then months and heartbreakingly the months became a year, then years. Years of endless meetings, court sessions that promised results. Results that raised our hopes; but results that were meaningless when overturned by another court; a court with different laws, with a different culture and different beliefs. They were years of not knowing, but forever loving. We sent letters and photos, stories about home, presents and cards, but we never knew if they reached her. Sarah kept on with her job, she had to show that she could provide a secure home. I carried on with my life as best I could. Both of us avoided friends with young children, unable to share the joy of Ipad images of smiling youngsters. We just kept going. We had to believe that one day we would win and she would come home.

Today we are finally at the airport. It is taking all our strength to hang on to that belief. We can hardly talk to each other. The arrivals hall gets busy, and then empties as flights touchdown and passengers pour through the doors of the customs hall. It is still another hour before the flight is due. We stand at the barrier scanning the faces, watching the arrivals board. I fetch coffee in paper cups that neither of us wants. Sunburnt holidaymakers laugh and shout 'look at the weather!' as they pull their suitcases towards the exit. A young man offers us a seat but we prefer to stand. Pacing slightly from left to right, we want to hold on to our position facing the arrivals doors. We don't want to waste a single second. We are waiting for a young girl, last seen as a toddler, now a teenager. I shut my eyes. 'Please God let it be OK'. I try to relax, push my hands into my pocket, finger the little welcome present that I have chosen so carefully.

The plane should have left by now. I jump as Sarah's phone rings and grab her arm. I am watching every movement of her face as she answers it.

I am watching as she presses the phone to her ear, her knuckles as white as her face. I can hardly breathe. I am watching as the tears gather in the corners of her eyes and spill down her cheeks. Then I hear her whispered, 'thank you.'

Erica Guise

Farm Elegy

Behind the barn
rickety wooden sheep-pens have been erased.
Now it's landscaped gardens,
clipped hedges, a statue of a nymph
in a half-filled bowl of water,
only one Victoria plum tree left.

The loft is converted into a flat.
I imagine it smells vanilla fresh.
Restful photographs in black and white,
of tractors, hay on trailers, capped farmers,
hang on the walls, orchids made with wire
and silk rest on a spruce table.

No stately cows jostle by the gate.
No sheep graze in the fields.
The stable where the sheepdog slept
is part of an extended kitchen,
Aga-bright and dishwasher safe.
The land that slopes down to the river is quiet.

Cathy Whittaker
Published in Quintet and other Poets Cinnamon Press

A Springtime Tale or Much Ado About Shakespeare

Now are the citizens of Stratford gathered in the streets made glorious festive by the flags and flowers. Mighty dignitaries march forth in finery, their ceremonial chains glister in the struggling sun. Strangely for this Earth, this soggy isle, this England, the rain it raineth not today. The solemn sonorous bell tolls as the bier passeth along the streets, with rosemary for remembrance thrown in its path. The yellow Shakespeare banner unfolds in tardy fashion marking four hundred years since he did depart this life. The playwright's quill presented by a fresh-faced lad to the heaving multitude.

Whereupon it is decreed ten thousand masks be donned - each a like resemblance of the Bard. Though this be madness, yet there is method in't. An inclusion in the mighty Guinness Book of Records is the avowed intent. The red-faced, portly Cryer in loud persuasion entreats the crowd - 'Hip, Hip Hooray - Friends, tourists and Stratfordians send up your cheers.' This followed by the anthem to our noble Queen.

Out sounds a shot. A shower of glitter is disposed, it droppeth as a gentle dew from Heaven. Some get nothing. Some receive pieces of yellow and black paper confetti and some have golden shiny streamers thrust upon them. Alas poor Peter, husband mine, wherefore art thou? Thou hast been unsighted for this past hour. No good ensues from oft uncharged mobiles.

But what's afoot? We wait the Band of New Orleans to lead us to the Church. But murmur, murmur, whisper, whisper, now a rumour suggests the band pass not along our way. To go or not to go, that is the question. Whether 'tis better to chance a sighting or to leg it to Holy Trinity perchance to catch them there. This crowd, this happy bustling crowd doth block our path and murder easy passage. Oh, that their too too solid flesh would melt. We are decided. So go we through Debenhams with all good speed to Rother Street and Chestnut Walk. Here find we a goodly number assembled, but not in mass so deep as to inhibit vision. A few, a happy few, partaking of a quantity of wine, offer salutations as we achieve the Holy Pile.

Thus pass us in a great parade all manner of men and women. Strange tongued travellers from other Stratford towns in distant and then undiscovered lands: Australia, New Zealand, Thailand, Canada and the United States. Schoolboys with their satchels and shining faces. Marching men, with dolorous drums, fluting pipes and harsh blown trumpets, lead:

masonic magnates, a throng of thespians, the worshipful Company of Fruiterers, bewigged lawyers, black gowned academics and a merry pair purporting to be the Bard and his wife.

And lo, at last, cometh the long awaited clamorous, raucous, jubilant music of the New Orleans Band. We shall not look upon its like again in this place. All announce their worth by pennants and sport fragrant flowers of many colours to place at the grave of William Shakespeare. A man whose plays would sound as sweet if penned by any other name, but Shakeshaft, Warwickshire Will, the Upstart Crow, in Shakespeare's County, we own, cherish and salute you. This man, this noble genius who in his time wrote many plays is oft remembered, but never more than today, when the plays the thing, Stratford a stage and all the goodly joyous throng, merely players.

Methinks slothful grandchildren in Welford, now abed, will think themselves accursed they were not here with us on this St. Georges Day. Cry God for Shakespeare, England and St George.

Written to commemorate the 400th Anniversary of the death of Shakespeare, which was celebrated with enthusiasm and panache in Stratford Upon Avon on 23rd April 2016.

Mary Sylvester

A Perfect Profile

Uninvited, the image of a handsome young man projected itself into Agamina's mind.

'Stop it Mum.'

'Yannick's perfect,' she heard the insistent echo of her mother's voice tagged to the image. 'He has a 99.7% positive genetic correlation; projected earnings capacity of 2.5bn Galactic; and a reproductive probability profile forecasting four children – 2.1 female and 1.9 male.'

Agamina sighed.

'Well, what's wrong with him?' The voice in Agamina's head insisted.

'I'm sure there's nothing wrong with him Mum. It's just...'

'It's just what?'

'Well, it's just not the right time.'

She gazed out through the plasma window where Pasha and some of the other men were playing an impromptu game of football. They had taken off their Protec jackets and were using them as makeshift goalposts. Even though the plasma window noise filter was at maximum, she could hear the happy strains of shouts and laughter.

'I hope you haven't done anything foolish Aggie.'

'Don't be ridiculous Mum.' Agamina moved away from the window.

'I just want you to be happy.'

'I know.'

Agamina turned as a louder shout than normal reached her. Pasha was holding his hands up in triumph, having scored a decisive goal. The voices faded. The men picked up their jackets, shaking hands and slapping each other on the back.

'You should never have left Antares. Spending your life digging up old bones. What good is that I ask you?'

'But Mum this is such an opportunity. We're involved in ground breaking research here. It's going to change our view of how human societies evolved. All the theories of human migration through the Universe are going to have to be rewritten.'

'You could have had a career at AGU. Professor Mattissen said as much.'

Agamina pictured the ceramic towers of Antares Global University. It was true she had been fortunate to go there: the leading university in the galaxy, academically rigorous, the finest minds, and a gateway to a career in the cognosphere. As the centre of the known Universe, Antares itself had everything: home to the senate, intergalactic banking, the highest life expectancy anywhere; with care, she should live to celebrate her three hundredth birthday. Perhaps she should have stayed on, but it felt…felt what? Sterile somehow, bloodless and unexciting. Everything was predictable, calculated, stifling. She looked out to see Pasha and the others heading back to the dig, his shoulders silhouetted in the afternoon sun. She moved over to her desk and peered at some of the objects they had uncovered that morning.

'Look Mum, I'd better get back to work.'

'Well what do you want to do about Yannick?'

'Let me think about it Mum.'

'Don't think about it too long. He has a profile to die for.'

'OK Mum. Love you.'

Agamina touched her temple and the hum of the holographic imager faded. She put on her Protec gloves and picked up the small rectangular shaped object she had been working on. A capsule of some sort. She put on a magnetic field face mask, picked up a sonic brush, set the oscillation to minimum and started to clear away the surface dirt. A small pile of dust built up in the collecting tray. The object was clearly made of some rudimentary material, possibly hydrocarbon based. She peered through the face mask at some lettering that began to appear '16GB'. She held the lettering up to the computer sensor.

'Archive search.' The sensor rotated to focus on the lettering.

'Possible twenty-fifth century text for computer data storage capacity,' the sensor spoke in soft dull tones, 'probability eighty-five percent.'

Agamina stared at the capsule. A computer storage disk then; '16GB' presumably sixteen gigabytes. Could anything be stored in such a small capacity?

'Data download,' she said.

The sensor moved closer to touch the capsule in her hand. She looked up at the plasma screen to see if any transfer of data was possible. A stream of images started to appear.

'Security check.' No point in taking any risks.

The screen froze as the data security check started. It would be amazing to find data from the twenty-fifth century. She looked at the capsule. Hard to believe that this wasn't human in origin. It looked like some of the rare specimens she had seen at the Antares Central Museum, although this had to be at least two thousand years older. She placed the capsule gently on the tray, the sensor followed her movement.

'Security check clear,' the computer said.

'Show data.'

The images resolved on the plasma screen. A film of some sort.

'Translation.'

The sensor whirred.

'Early Anglo-Frisian similar to twenty-eighth century Alpha Centauri scripts.' The dull monotone of the sensor at odds with the fast beating of Agamina's heart. This could be it. The Holy grail they were looking for. The translation kicked in. The film was a documentary referring back to earlier documentaries. A grainy image of a man and a veiled person, presumably a woman, appeared.

'In Eastern societies, arranged marriages were common. It was believed that parental selection of wives was likely to result in a better marital outcome. In practice the motives for these marriages were either financial or for social advancement. The practice was made illegal on Earth after the Religious Wars of the twenty-second century.'

The image broke up.

'What happened?' Agamina asked.

'Data corrupted.'

'Can it be corrected?'

'Working.' The sensor went silent.

Agamina stood back from the observation table and took her mask and gloves off. She stood by the plasma window, but Pasha and the others were out of sight. She glanced back at the frozen image on the plasma screen. The veiled figure in the shadow of the man.

After supper, she would ask Pasha if he would like to go for a walk. She smiled. She could already feel the invigorating Sol 3 atmosphere in her lungs.

Paul Budd

Flanders' Silent Tunnels

We do not hear the enemy approach
nor the priming of the mine.
The constant tap of our shovels
replaced by the pounding
of our blood.

The earth is heavy
on my back as I lie here,
damp clay sour in my mouth.

For a moment I am with you,
warm in our marriage bed,
the blanket light on my body,
your skin sweet and soft,
your voice comforting,
'Come home to me soon my love.'

I know my mate and I
must wait
for the rescue party
to dig us an exit.
I fear it is too late.
Earth's blanket has him
trapped and bound.

Please forgive me, my love.
I am a tunneller.
I cannot leave my mate.

Julie Fulton

Standing on Ceremony

The man stepped out of the lift into the foyer of the hotel. It was bursting at the seams with people; the men were handsome, the women beautiful. Glasses tinkled. There was laughter everywhere. Furtive sidelong glances took in what people were wearing and who they were with. Noise levels intense. Everyone talked at once.

The man was dressed in black tie and immaculately pressed tuxedo. His white shirt spotless, his hair neatly combed and his face recently shaven. A casual bystander wouldn't have noticed him. He looked the same as everyone else. But there was a crucial difference - he was a gatecrasher.

He made his way, unhurried, into the crowd. He checked, once again, the huge black notice board that stood alongside the reception desk to make sure he was in the right place.

> *'Maluda Franks Merchant Bank*
> *Cocktails from 19.00 in the Garden Room*
> *Reception followed by Dinner 20.00 in the Waterloo Chamber.*
> *Annual Awards Ceremony to follow'*

He looked around taking in the buzz, the high level of excitement and expectation. This was the best part of the evening. Later, when the awards were announced, there would be only disappointment for many. But for now, hope was still alive and one could sense the butterflies of anticipation and hoped for success.

Shaking his head as if clearing his mind of what he knew, he turned to one of the nearby attendants who was carrying, above his shoulder, a large tray containing flutes of champagne that bubbled and sparkled as they caught the light from the exquisite chandeliers.

'May I?' he asked.

'Certainly, sir,' said the sommelier, bringing the tray down so that the man could reach one of the glasses.

'Thank you,' he said, just as he appeared to catch sight of someone in another part of the room.

'Ah!' he called out, smiling broadly. 'There you are! Over here!'

He put up his free hand and waved to no-one in particular.

'I'd better take another one of those'

'By all means, sir,' said the waiter once again offering the tray before turning away to serve a group of new arrivals.

The man knew about champagne and carried the two glasses very carefully. Maluda Franks spared no expense on these occasions and this was bubbly of the highest quality. It would be inexcusable to spill any.

He spotted a side table alongside a convenient pillar behind which he would be well-nigh invisible to anyone curious enough to take an interest in him.

He put the flutes down on the table and then stood back to admire the quality and excellence of the crystal. After a moment, he reached into the inside pocket of his jacket and took out a small package of pills. He counted them to be sure – there were eight as he knew there would be. Slowly, he dropped four of the tablets into one of the glasses and watched as they dissolved and fizzed like antacid in water. He put the glass to his lips and drank it back in one. For a split second, there was regret, at not savouring the bouquet, but it was too late for all of that.

He took a deep breath and did the same with the second glass.

He felt the warmth of the alcohol and the drugs as they entered his bloodstream. In his mind's eye, he saw them floating around his body, doing their damage, and taking away the pain and humiliation.

 He waited a moment and then burped very loudly.

'Oh, pardon me!' he said and then laughed because no-one could hear him.

He looked at the empty glasses and took the letter out of his pocket.

He put it on the small table and, for the last time, caught sight of the words that had changed his life. 'Regret', 'having to let you go'. Nothing unusual, words that one might use every day; but for him, the end of everything he'd known: his job, lifestyle, marriage; all gone in the twinkling of an eye or in a single bubble of this champagne.

With astonishing speed, he'd become Yesterday's Man – confirmed with a cruel sharpness - when he'd walked amongst the assembled crowds tonight completely unrecognised.

He it was who, on so many of these evenings in the past, had been on the receiving end of awards and citations in acknowledgement of his long and dedicated service to Maluda Franks Merchant Bank. He thought it fitting, therefore, that it should be here that he brought it to a conclusion.

Lying down on the floor, he closed his eyes, grateful for the privacy. He was surprised that he felt quite comfortable and then, before too long, there was nothing.

Margaret Ward

Out in the Midday Sun

Bright red poinsettias sparkled in the sun. It was midday and the heat was oppressive.

'Do be careful Harry.' I could feel the fear in my mother's voice. Anyway, I didn't need to be told about the dangers of a dog with rabies. Everyone had heard of the consequences of being bitten by these poor creatures; you didn't live in Bangkok without hearing about someone who had the fifty daily anti rabies injections that followed contact with them. Fifty daily anti-rabies injections into your stomach, not to mention the anxiety that it might be too late. Dogs were not regarded as man's best friend, rather as a potentially lethal health hazard and generally avoided at all costs.

Our house was built on sturdy pillars, no glass at the windows, only shutters and mosquito nets. It was in a large compound which also contained Christ Church, Bangkok, an Anglican Church in the centre of a Buddhist country. A drive circled the church. A drive I used to stagger around on stilts, ride my tricycle and later my bike.

My mother and I leant out of the sitting room window, watching as my father and the gardener climbed into our little black Morris Minor. Slowly, the gardener drove close to the poor animal. My father cautiously opened the car door armed only with a large stick. I saw my mother's knuckles whiten as they gripped the window ledge. The stick rose and fell; the suffering beast was finally out of its misery.

As a countryman and lover of animals, it must have been hard to do, but most of all, very brave. I felt no horror at the death of the dog, only immense relief that my father was safe and that the danger was past.

Mary Sylvester

Water Torture

I cannot stand the sound of running water,
I cannot bear the noise of it all –
all these pretty brooks and streams
invade my peaceful dreams
and stretch my fragile nerves beyond recall.

While others sing the delights of rushing rivers
and plashing droplets falling into pools,
I voice my drowning fears
and cover up my ears
and I know that I must seem the worst of fools

Leave under running tap say the instructions,
well with me a quick splash is all they're going to get.
While I am busy wincing
and abbreviate their rinsing,
my lettuce leaves are lucky to get wet.

Come see the waterfalls say travel brochures,
Let running water lull you off to sleep –
they cannot have an inkling
that this incessant tinkling
awakens fears primeval and quite deep.

Niagara Falls are beautiful, I grant you,
amazing views from every side abound,
lovely by day or night,
an awe inspiring sight –
if only they could just turn off the sound.

I know all this ever moving water is a wonder,
it powers industry and is life force for all,
it is colourful, inspiring,
it draws many a glance admiring
from Severn Bore to China and Nepal.

Who sleeps within the sound of running water
has dreams beyond compare if I recall –
well whether clear or muddy
it's just not for me buddy
and if you're like me, you go quietly up the wall.

Gwen Zanzottera

Frances, Sister, Friend…

Frances was sad. Everyone could see it. Most people thought she was unhappy, but a few considered her unapproachable, standoffish. Others said she thought deeply, too deeply. Those who decided she was sad, wanted to know the reason why. Was her life full of regrets? If so, what were these regrets? She didn't talk about them. If you met up with her, she would acknowledge your presence but never tell you how she was feeling, you just got the idea that there was something wistful about her, something different.

Some people remembered her as a child, she had been quiet then, but not as much as now. She had a sister, Rosie, a year or so younger than her, and they were always together. Rosie was full of life, it was as though sunshine radiated from her. People were attracted to her. They gravitated towards the sisters, and Rosie especially would welcome them into their circle. There was always lots of noise and laughter. But one day Rosie wasn't there anymore. Frances was just the same as she had always been, or so people thought. She remained quiet, not attracting others particularly, no outward signs of change, but if you took the time to be with her, you could notice a subtle change in her demeanour. It was difficult to spot as she had always been one of a pair, she was the moon not the sun, the faded image.

I tried to find out what had happened to Rosie, but no-one would speak about it. One minute she was there and the next she wasn't. Frances carried on as normal. She existed, not sparkling, not anything. Every so often she could be seen deep in thought, no expression on her face but there was a hint of something in her eyes: sadness tinged with regret, but haughtiness as well. It made me wonder what she had done, she must have had something to do with Rosie's disappearance, I was sure of it.

I took to watching her, looking where she went. On the very rare occasions that she spoke, I listened intently. I wanted to get to know her more and to find out what had happened. I was sure there was something. When I tried to speak to her, I could see real fear in her eyes. She knew something but she was not going to let anything slip. I hoped that by staying close I would catch her in an unguarded moment, then all would be revealed. What I would do with the information, Heaven only knows. But I had to find out, it was as if it was eating away at me. I was becoming obsessed. What I thought I knew and what I wanted to know was taking over my every thought. I started to put likely scenarios together, they were becoming so real that I began to believe them.

Today Frances was unusually talkative, almost friendly. She talked about us going somewhere; a special place that she knew. She called me Rosie. I didn't think anything of it at the time, I was more interested in getting her to open up, I really thought this was it, I had broken through the ice, that she would finally tell me. That was my mistake, I let my guard down, didn't see what was coming. It's so dark, I don't even remember how I got here. There's no way out, no door that I can feel. The floor is damp and cold. Scratched in the stone beside my head are some marks, letters R O S I E.

Barbara Smith

Love and Lust on the Farm

Nancy was adorable. I loved her to bits. But she was a bit of a wild child and at the earliest opportunity, she left her mother's care. I knew what had happened as soon as I saw her in the hay loft that morning.

It was Sandy, of course. No one could deny that he was one sexy, alpha male, ginger haired, big, good looking, with a nice personality. He was one for the ladies, there was no two ways about it. The trouble was, he was a lot older than her, and although we all knew who her mother was, no one knew who the father had been. I had always suspected it might be Sandy.

So, when I went into the hay loft, and found her curled up with Sandy on top of the hay, my heart sank. Unless I was wrong, we had a case of incest on our hands. But what could I do? Her own mother had no control over her.

Of course, the inevitable happened. No sooner did her stomach begin to swell than Sandy chucked her out. I'm not sure how Nancy coped, or where she slept most nights. I offered her as much support as I could, but there wasn't much I could do, I was still at school at the time. When the babies were born, they were every bit as gorgeous as their mother.

Yes, I said babies. She had twins, a boy and a girl. They had their father's good looks, the boy was ginger haired. They were healthy and happy. Nancy was an excellent mother.

A woman from the village came to the door one day, delivering the parish magazine. As soon as she caught sight of the twins, she fell in love with them and asked about adopting them. Maybe she knew how overrun with babies we were. Nancy was still feeding them at that time, but to my consternation, my mother, said: yes, as soon as they were weaned, she could have them.

It was a sad day when the twins left, but we had to face facts, they would have a far better life with the parish magazine lady than Nancy or I could give them. Sure enough, they had all their inoculations, were soon growing, and loved their new home.

As for Nancy? Well, she didn't waste much time. Sandy took her back and she soon presented us with another litter of kittens.

Senga Hawker

My Father

His last breath breathed a gentle sigh
as if his spirit now could fly
to new adventure - God his guide.
As he had lived, my father died

A boy, his parents let him roam
the countryside became his home
to school a donkey he would ride.
As he had lived, my father died

From Oxford, distant lands appealed
Australia's raw charm revealed
five years all comfort put aside.
As he had lived, my father died.

In war to Aden he was sent.
In peace married his love in Ghent.
In death, my mother by his side
as he had lived, my father died.

Now with a child to the Far East,
to Christ Church, Bangkok as their priest,
all nationalities, no divide.
As he had lived, my father died.

From Devon with its red earthed tors,
the Midlands loved despite its flaws.
Here grandchildren became his pride.
As he had lived, my father died.

Then Somerset retired he went,
but still a helping hand he lent
until at 90, age defied.
As he had lived, my father died.

Last week he told his oldest friend
'I am dying. This is the end.'
So calm, accepting, nought denied,
as he had lived, my father died.

No illnesses until the last,
no secret sorrows in his past.
Joy, humour, wit and fun allied.
As he had lived, my father died

His last breath breathed - a gentle sigh,
as if his spirit now could fly
to new adventure - God his guide.
As he had lived, my father died.

Mary Sylvester

Understand this

He stands by the worn sofa, back to the window. I'd meant to clean the glass. The greasy mark's still there, glistening a warning in the morning sun.

'Roo,' he says, 'Roo, we can't do this anymore. It has to end - now.'

His hand, black and blue from last night, reaches for his mobile. He turns to look through the window, rubbing at the smears without seeing them, fingers sliding out of control. 'You have to understand.'

No, I think, *you have to understand.*

I won't let him do it. I walk to the kitchen, pick up the frying pan, unwashed after our last meal, return to the living room. His call remains unconnected. The thud of pan against skull makes Carly cry. I jog her up and down on my hip, the place she has been almost every minute since she came to me. She quietens.

I pick up the phone and end the call. 'We'll be fine,' I murmur into her ear. 'We'll go to the coast. They won't find us.'

Her parents will be fine too. It said on the news that they have other children. Not like me. I didn't have another to replace mine - until Carly.

I look at him sprawled on the floor. Blood trickles from his ears, darker than the tears that ran from the eyes of Carly's parents when I watched them on the telly.

Oh well, we all have to lose someone, sometime.

Julie Fulton

Broken Promises

I once thought that there had to be boundaries.
But you broke that golden concept.
Time and again I picked up the pieces.
I once thought there had to be boundaries.
Now I no longer pick up the pieces.
I had hoped you would learn to accept.
I once thought there had to be boundaries.
But you broke that golden concept.

Hazel Cross

Sugar Lumps

'Would you like sugar?' he asked, holding up the sugar bowl and helping himself to two lumps.

She shook her head. 'Since when did you start having sugar?' she asked.

'I can have sugar if I want to.'

She looked down at her hands. 'I didn't say you couldn't. I just wondered when you started taking sugar in coffee, that's all.'

'What difference does it make if I have sugar or not?'

She stared at him for a moment. 'Well, you never used to take sugar.'

'I did before I met you.' He dropped the lumps into his coffee from some height.

'Well, when did you stop?'

'For heaven's sake, will you stop going on about the sugar. I happen to like sugar in coffee.'

'You never said you did.'

'You never asked.'

She sighed and took a sip of coffee. 'I suppose I never knew you.'

'And what exactly is that supposed to mean?'

'You know very well,' she said, taking another sip.

'No I don't,' he said, stirring his coffee vigorously. 'What exactly do you mean?'

'Oh, nothing, let's not go on about it.' She glanced over toward the service counter.

'I'm not the one going on about it.'

She placed her cup on its saucer. 'Yes, you are,' she said.

'You're the one who brought up about the sugar.'

'Well, I never knew you liked sugar in coffee. Just another thing to add to the list.'

His shoulders slumped. 'Oh, don't start. We agreed not to go over old ground.'

'I'm not starting.' She paused. 'Anyway, if you want to ruin your teeth it's up to you.'

'It absolutely is up to me.'

She turned the cup in its saucer. 'Well, I agree with you. Show's we can agree on something.' She paused. 'Anyway, it's not going to be me worrying about your teeth, is it?'

'Look, let's leave it. I don't think it's taking us anywhere, do you?' He stood up and went over to the till.

Paul Budd

Doctor's Orders

As he looked at the name in front of him on the computer screen, Tom gripped his hands together under the desk and braced himself. He heard the footsteps as they came down the corridor, followed by the customary short tap and then the familiar face peered round the door of his surgery.

'Good morning, Doctor!'

'Oh, yes …Good morning, Mrs Harris,' he said, looking up. 'What a surprise. We haven't seen you since.…er, last Tuesday'

'That's right Doctor, you know I hate to bother you when it isn't necessary'.

Tom indicated to the chair alongside him and she sat down.

'Quite so, Mrs Harris. Well, here you are so … what I can I do for you today?'

He glanced across, before returning to scrutinise something that appeared to be of momentous importance on his computer.

'Doctor, you're going to be so surprised – you'll never believe it'

'Try me, Mrs Harris.' He moved the mouse around as if to highlight something.

'I've got the most wonderful news.'

'Let me guess, you're moving back to Cork to be nearer your sister? I know you've been talking of this ever since Mr Harris passed away.'

Tom hoped his enthusiasm for this possible course of action wasn't too obvious.

Mrs Harris first put her shopping bag down on the floor, grasped her handbag to her chest and then finally, settled in.

'Oh, I couldn't do that now, Doctor, there's too much at stake. And, you know, I've lived here for such a long time that I'm probably bilingual.'

'Bilingual, Mrs Harris?'

She leaned forward.

'Oh Yes, Doctor, haven't you ever heard of it? It's when you're a bit of this and a bit of that. So, you see, in my case, even though I'm still Irish, I love 'EastEnders' and Pancake Tuesday and I'm *very* fond of the Queen so I suppose I'm English as well.'

Tom moved his computer from one side of the desk to the other.

'I see, Mrs Harris'

'Besides I've just been reading in that magazine 'Mother and Baby', that you have in the Waiting Room, that expectant mothers should try to stay with the same doctor until their confinement and …'

'Now just steady on a moment, Mrs Harris. Whose confinement are we talking about?'

'Mine, Doctor; I'm pregnant.'

Tom turned away from the screen, and looked across at his patient whilst attempting to keep a neutral expression on his face.

'Did you say 'pregnant', Mrs Harris?'

'I did Doctor'

'Mrs Harris, I think you need to listen to me very carefully'

'I always do, Doctor,' she said, as she pulled her chair a little closer.

'Mrs Harris, you are widowed, you are 72 years old and, I'm sure as I can be about anything, you are not in receipt of IVF treatment!'

'Now, now, Doctor! You always did tend to pour cold water on things.'

He could hear his voice rising.

'I can't put this any more strongly, Mrs Harris. The likelihood of you being pregnant is not only beyond the bounds of possibility but, if you will pardon the pun, inconceivable!'

'Oh Doctor, you are funny! Still, it wouldn't be the first time this has happened, would it?'

'It would in my experience, Mrs Harris……. and there are certain essential requirements needed if one is to become pregnant, aren't there, for example, ……'

'Please, Doctor don't mention… you know, that word! I always get squeamish when anybody talks about 'it'. You see, my late husband was a perfect gentleman and never raised the subject because he knew how it affected me.'

'Are you saying that you and Mr Harris didn't ever…?'

Tom noticed her looking rather warily at the examination couch in the corner of the room.

'Let me put it this way Doctor' she said, pushing her chair a little further away from him, 'He never asked and I never offered and we got along very nicely, thank you very much. But this is quite different'

'How is it different, Mrs Harris?'

Tom now abandoned his computer screen – there was nothing there to help him with this one - he was on his own.

'Do you read the Bible, Doctor?'

'Uumm, I suppose if I'm being honest, not very often – but what's this leading up to, Mrs Harris? Have you been praying for a baby?'

She moved her chair towards him once more.

'No, Doctor – but sometimes God works in very mysterious ways. Take the case of Cousin Elizabeth.'

'Cousin Elizabeth? Whose cousin? I thought you were telling me something about the bible.'

'I *am*, Doctor! According to the bible, Mary went to visit her cousin who was called Elizabeth. When she got there, she discovered that her cousin, who was over seventy, was having a baby. Have you heard about this?'

In desperation, he turned back to his computer screen in the vain hope it would point him in the direction of this particular bible story.

'Yes, I think I have now that you mention it. But what does this have to do with …. ah! oh I see… Mrs Harris, are you perhaps suggesting that this pregnancy of yours has come about under similar circumstances?'

'Yes, Doctor, I am. A woman knows these things, doesn't she?'

He wondered if they should just exchange places so that she could tell *him* what next to do.

'Right Mrs Harris! Please tell me – how long have you had these symptoms that have led you to believe you were pregnant?'

'Only since this morning – so I thought I'd better come and see you straight away.'

'And what were they?'

'I felt a bit off, you know, a bit queasy when I got up. Then I remembered Cousin Elizabeth – I was reading about her yesterday.'

He closed his eyes and ran his fingers through his hair trying not to tear it out.

Mrs Harris pulled a face and started rummaging in her handbag.

'Doctor, now will you look at what you've done to your hair - its standing on end and I haven't got a comb with me! Do you have one, Doctor, you look very bedraggled!'

He ignored her.

'What did you have to eat last night, Mrs Harris?'

'I had a piece of fish – and I have to say it wasn't very nice. I shall have to have a word with that young chap at the fishmongers.'

'And that's it? Feeling a bit queasy this morning and reading about Cousin Elizabeth yesterday?'

'Yes, Doctor.'

'Well, Mrs Harris, I suggest you don't go out and spend all your money on baby clothes. You see, you are not pregnant - you have a slight tummy upset - most likely that fish you ate last night.'

His computer screen shone out to him like a port in a storm.

'Oh, is that so Doctor? Well, that's a little disappointing, I must say. On the other hand, I suppose having a baby would have been a bit awkward. I wouldn't have wanted to miss my day trips and things like that. Yes, it's probably for the best – my cat wouldn't have liked it either – he's a bit set in his ways. And, something else was already worrying me, Doctor - what the baby should be called. You see, my Christian name and surname happen to rhyme with each other – Clarice Harris - and I thought it would be quite nice to carry this on. A name that was similar but different. And then, lo and behold, this morning, whilst making a cup of tea, 'Yaris' came into my head. What do you think of that, Doctor? Right out of the blue it came to me – Yaris Harris. But then, almost straight away, I had second thoughts as I began to have a funny feeling that Yaris is the name of a car. Am I right, Doctor?'

'I really don't know, Mrs Harris.'

He was now moving his mouse around so fast it fell on the floor.

She bent to pick it up at the same time he did and they almost collided.

'Well, thank goodness I don't have to worry about names anymore, Doctor. Things usually work out in the end, don't they? And, as the old saying goes - life is just a bowl of strawberries'

'Quite so', he said.

From the corner of his eye Tom saw her reaching down to gather up her shopping bag – the usual sign she was preparing to leave. As an overwhelming sense of relief washed over him, he began to rise slowly from his chair in the hope she would follow suit. However, despite his euphoria he knew from experience that he still needed to be careful. This was always the tricky part, getting her to the door of the surgery and outside again, back on to the corridor.

'I'm glad you've taken it so well, Mrs Harris; and if your tummy doesn't clear up in a day or two – why not come back and see Doctor Fletcher? He's very good with tummies.'

'It's very kind of you to advise me to see another doctor especially if he's an expert - but, I'm very loyal and wouldn't dream of doing such a thing. I've always had great faith in you and I'll ask for you as always when I come again. Now please don't stand, Doctor, you know I don't stand on ceremony – ooh now that's a joke… stand… stand on ceremony! Ha! Ha! Yes. I don't usually tell jokes maybe I'll have to start doing it more often.'

'Good bye Mrs Harris …'

'Oh Doctor, I've just thought of something else'

'Please don't sit down again, Mrs Harris …'

'I won't keep you a moment longer than I need to. Do you think it's possible that I might have appendicitis? Perhaps I should have a prescription? I don't like telling you what to do but I have a lot of experience of illness as you know and it's better to nip things in the bud… what do you say Doc… Ooh – now, why are you doing that? Why are you banging your head on the desk? You're going to hurt yourself and then what would I do?'

Margaret Ward

First Love

He said I'll love you always and for ever I'll be true
and we carved our initials on a tree, the way that lovers do.
He gave me such unusual gifts to prove his love for me
and I treasured them in a covered box, and hid it carefully.

He said I'll love you always and you are the only one,
and that summer everything was bright, the days so full of fun.
We spent our perfect evenings walking slowly hand in hand
across fields and over bridges and along wavy patterned sand.

He said I'll love you always and you are my true ideal,
and no one can ever understand exactly how I feel.
We had picnics in the hedgerows and we shared a sticky Mars,
and we exchanged chaste youthful kisses, standing underneath the stars.

But he lied to me, my hero, and when summer days had gone
so had he, back to his city, leaving me here all alone,
with a covered box of daisy chains, a woven bracelet and a ring
made out of an old coke pull, which to me meant everything

He said I'll love you always, but that always was two weeks,
and his lies shattered my youthful heart, took the roses from my cheeks.
This first love, achingly beautiful, left me bereft, with pillow damp
as I cried for my lying Lothario, whom I met at a summer camp.

Gwen Zanzottera

Laura

Laura shut down the computer and watched the screen flicker from blue to black. She was happy with the e-mails she had sent. Such a different world from the one she had been born into.

In the kitchen, she cleared the work surface, returned the bread to the bread bin and the butter to the fridge. From the dresser drawer, she took the typed papers and documents and slipped them into a large manila envelope. She used the Schaeffer pen with the italic nib to write her granddaughter's name in copperplate. She placed the envelope in the centre of the kitchen table. From the cupboard, she took a crystal whisky glass and half filled it with tap water. She counted out four of the sleeping tablets prescribed by her doctor and put them one at a time onto her tongue. With each she took a sip of water and swallowed. She replaced the white cap on the brown medicine bottle and put it to the back of the kitchen drawer.

In the utility room, she put on her green wellington boots, feeling the cold lining against her bare feet. She picked up her walking stick and the old tartan picnic blanket and opened the door. The rush of cold air struck her face and she bent her head against the icy wind. She pulled the door, feeling the familiar click of the latch through the handle. With considerable effort, she walked through the snow-covered grass and into the big meadow. She walked and walked, following the line of the river bank. She did not look back. When she was too tired and too cold to walk any further she knelt down and spread the blanket as best she could over the soft snow. She felt the darn in the weave, repaired, she remembered on a lovely summer's day when the children were young. She lay down, looked up into the clear night sky, then closed her eyes. She turned onto her side and soon she was asleep.

Mary Durndell

102 Not Out

I hesitate in the doorway, waiting,
my fears and those unshed tears
    held back by an half-open door.

I stand in the doorway waiting
for a glimpse of an age-bent figure,
    now thin as the stick that supports it.

I stand in the doorway, hoping
for the shuffle of slippered feet,
    and a smile from a life-worn face.

I stand with my hand on the latch,
my lips holding words of greeting.
    But still I don't open that door.

I hesitate in the doorway waiting,
hoping I can say '*how are you today?*'
    …and not that inevitable last goodbye.

Erica Guise

Author Biographies

Paul Budd

Chartered Accountant and Banker turned author, Paul has an MA in Creative Writing from Oxford Brookes. He has published a novel and is working on a second. He lives in Worcestershire with his wife Mary.

Hazel Cross

In 1962 Hazel came to live in Worcestershire with her husband and young family. She taught for many years in Evesham. After retiring she became a volunteer for Guide Dogs, breeding puppies for the organisation in the garage. Around 2004 she helped start an informal writing group in her village and found she enjoyed sharing the fruits of the group's imaginations. Encouraged by this, in 2009 she joined a second group led by Cathy Whittaker. Over the years, she has learned a huge amount but still has lots to learn. She has also made a group of good friends into the bargain whose encouragement has made it fun!

Mary Durndell

Born in rural Buckinghamshire, Mary has always enjoyed writing, particularly memoir and creative non-fiction. Following her nursing and midwifery training, she qualified as a health visitor, and spent many years working in the community. She gained a master's degree in creative writing from Oxford Brookes in 2014 and is working on her first novel.

Julie Fulton

Julie lives in rural Worcestershire where she teaches music, sings, dances, writes, reads, grows vegetables and goes narrowboating - not necessarily all at the same time. She enjoys writing all sorts of things, but has a special love of poetry and children's stories. She has had some picture books published and is looking forward to seeing her new one in print in November 2017.

Erica Guise

Erica joined her first creative writing group in her early thirties. Then inevitably the demands of a growing family, with its numerous cats, dogs, and even a flock of sheep, all took precedence. It was to be thirty years and a lifetime of experiences later before another writing group beckoned. She is particularly interested in characterisation and relationships.

Senga Hawker

Senga was born in Scotland and had an ambition to write as a child, but was distracted by work and family commitments. After a career in local government, including a job as a housebound librarian, she is now intent on making up for lost time.

Barbara Smith

Barbara was born in Birmingham and now lives in Stratford upon Avon and Swanage with her husband. She has worked as a nurse and has had four books relating to nursing and health studies published.

Mary Sylvester

Mary Sylvester was born in London within the sound of Bow bells and therefore is technically a cockney. However, apart from the first six weeks, she spent her childhood in Bangkok (Thailand) and Devon. Sadly, her diary written aged nine, about the journey home from Bangkok in which the family visited numerous fascinating places, concentrated mainly on food. However, since joining a village writing group and subsequently Scribes, at last Mary is extending her writing subject matter and enjoying the experience.

Margaret Ward

Margaret was born and brought up in Lancashire. She moved to Worcestershire in 1986 and has lived there ever since. She is married with two children and three grandchildren. She worked as a relationship counsellor for many years and has been writing short stories and poetry for about ten years.

Cathy Whittaker

Cathy has had a sequence of fifteen poems published in *Quintet*, Cinnamon Press which are loosely based on her childhood in the Lake District. Her work has also appeared in *Under the Radar, Prole, The Interpreter's House, Envoi, Orbis, Ink Sweat & Tears, The Magnolia Review, Mslexia*, and many other magazines and anthologies. She was shortlisted for the Bridport Prize, 2015. She was chosen by Poetry on Loan for their West Midlands postcard series. Cathy is a tutor in Poetry, Memoir and Creative Writing at Percival Guildhouse, Rugby and for other groups. She also works with a colleague offering Creative Writing Workshops for various organisations; www.openmindwriting.com. She finds walking a good way to unwind and work on ideas for poems.

Gwen Zanzottera

A Cockney who went to Broadway, Worcestershire, to escape the blitz, she left school at eighteen and worked as a secretary in England and Dusseldorf. Changed direction at sixty-one to become a tour guide and recently retired after twenty-five years of going topless round Stratford upon Avon. Sang and acted in various amateur musicals, turned professional and is now a member of a group which does murder events. Has had stories and poems published and written two books on derivation of popular sayings.

Made in the USA
Columbia, SC
16 July 2017